This book belongs to

Jayden

For my children Kiana, Kinsley, and Landon.
Life will take you to places, some near and some far.
But remember, I'll love you — wherever you are.

Acknowledgements:
To my amazing team of creators and professionals:
Editor: Nicole Filippone, Illustrator: Gabby Correia, and Book Designer: Praise Saflor
Thank you for all you do. Your talents and creative skills are beyond extraordinary.

ISBN: 978-1-7351996-4-1 (Hardback)
978-1-7351996-3-4 (Paperback)
978-1-7351996-5-8 (E-book)

Library of Congress Control Number: 2021921420
Edited by Nicole Filippone
Illustrations by Gabby Correia
Book Design by Praise Saflor

First printing edition 2021

Colors on the Spectrum

www.sarinasiebenaler.com

DO NOT WISH FOR A BIRTHDAY UNICORN!

By Sarina Siebenaler
Illustrated by Gabby Correia

To Kat
From Marie
DECEMBER
SUN
MON
TUES
WED
THU
FRI
SAT
1 ask mom for unicorn
2 Send Birthday invites
3 Ballet
11 Trotter twins Playdate!
14 MY BIRTHDAY!
15 Gabby's Birthday!
17 Ballet
25 Christmas!
27 Ballet
KAT

Join us for
KAT'S
Magical BiRTHDAY
Date: Saturday, December 14th
Time: 1:00 p.m. sharp
Where: 179 W. Fun Circle Lane
Request: Wear bright colors.
Unicorns like that.
WHO TO INVITE
Sally Lee Crystal
Page Tom Paul
Raphaela
Melvin
Tyron
UNICORN

A birthday is special. It comes once a year.

It's a time to feel loved by the
ones we hold dear.

My mom said she'll grant me my wish for a theme.

A UNICORN party!

A FAIRYTALE dream!

She will shimmer and shine,
with her mane all aglow.
She'll be all that I've wished for
and be a grand show!

So, we looked up our options and read the reviews.

There were pink ones and

gold ones and

some with TATTOOS!

We finally found one — a glorious sight.
"Look, she's discounted too!" Mom exclaimed with

179

Then my grandma set off
to retrieve our new guest.
And she drove with great
caution while heading out west.

She was greeted by Stan, who was large and quite tan.
Then his crew strapped the unicorn to her sedan.

UNI
express

HAPPY BIRTHD
BIRTHDAY GIRL

It was finally time —
all my guests had appeared.
"Oh, please show us your unicorn!"
all of them cheered.

I excitedly watched as she made her debut...

But, uhhh, something was wrong...
was she sick with the flu?

Her long mane was a frazzle, her horn — it was chipped.
Her big eyes, dark and puffy, her hooves weren't clipped.

Not a shine to her nature, nor gleam in her eye,
she seemed lost and distressed — or just playfully shy?

We were so disappointed — we couldn't deny.
But we quickly felt sad when she started to cry.

We noticed a note in her tangled-up mane
and then eagerly read as it tried to explain.

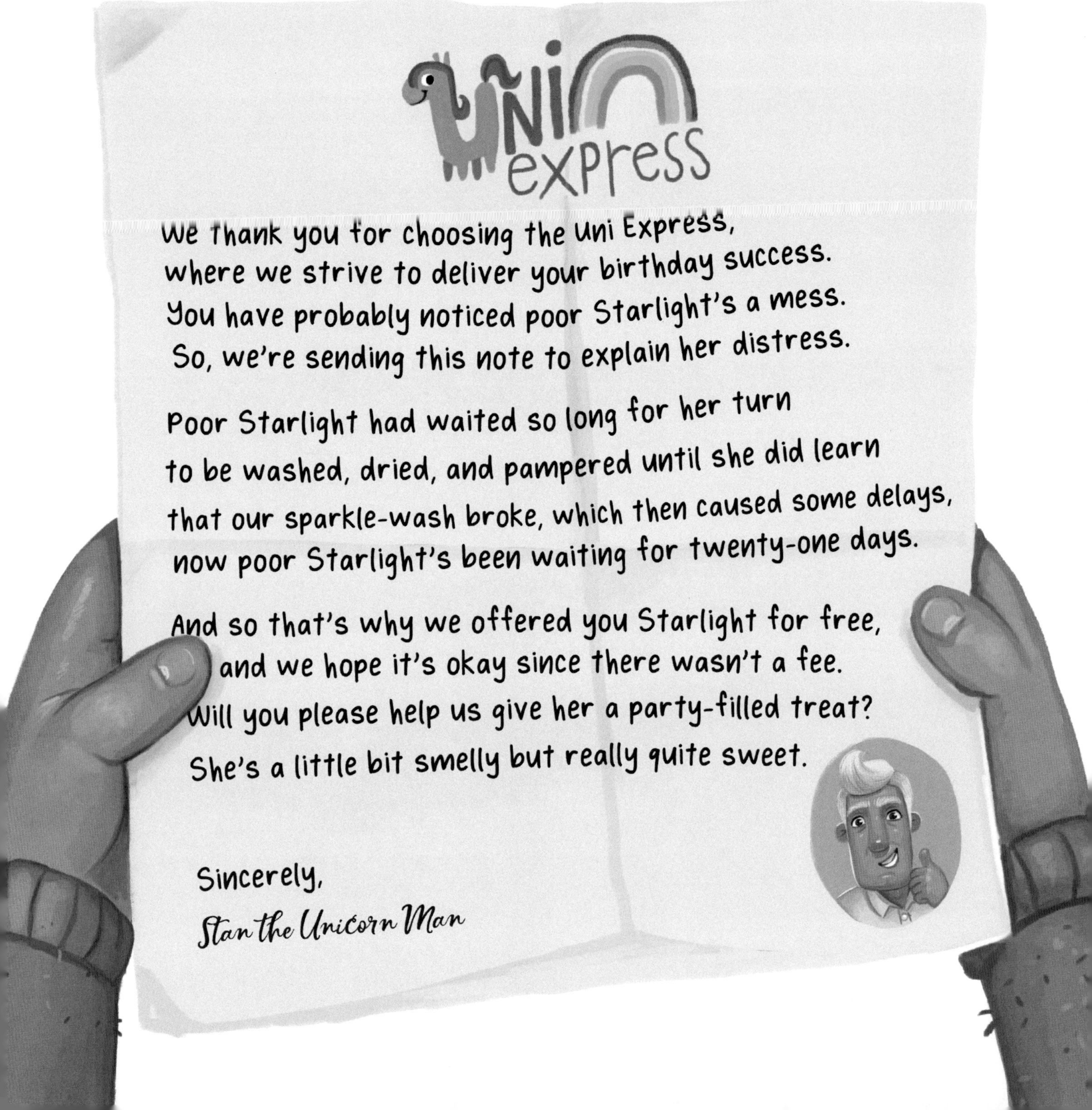

Uni Express

We thank you for choosing the Uni Express,
where we strive to deliver your birthday success.
You have probably noticed poor Starlight's a mess.
So, we're sending this note to explain her distress.

Poor Starlight had waited so long for her turn
to be washed, dried, and pampered until she did learn
that our sparkle-wash broke, which then caused some delays,
now poor Starlight's been waiting for twenty-one days.

And so that's why we offered you Starlight for free,
and we hope it's okay since there wasn't a fee.
Will you please help us give her a party-filled treat?
She's a little bit smelly but really quite sweet.

Sincerely,

Stan the Unicorn Man

WARNING
OUT OF ORDER
SPARKLE
WASH

Then our grandma called out,
"I'll return to the shop!
This is not what we ordered –
we'll do a quick swap!"

"Oh, but Grandma," I said,
"Starlight needs us right now.
We should think of a plan –
make her happy somehow."

We tried bouncing around in a house made of air,
but her horn pierced a hole, and it crumpled right there.

We played 'Try Not to Laugh,'
which has always worked well,
but poor Starlight stayed sad,
as if under a spell.

"Oh, I have an idea!
This plan will be great.
We will clean her right up –
it is still not too late."

HAPPY BIR
1
SPLASH
TANG FREE SHAMP
WHOOSH
2
POOF!
3
Sparkle
4

SHINE
5
OOPS!
6
7
WOW!
8
GREAT WORK!

"Oh, dear Starlight," we said,
"are you ready to see?
Please come out when you hear us
count one, two, and three!"

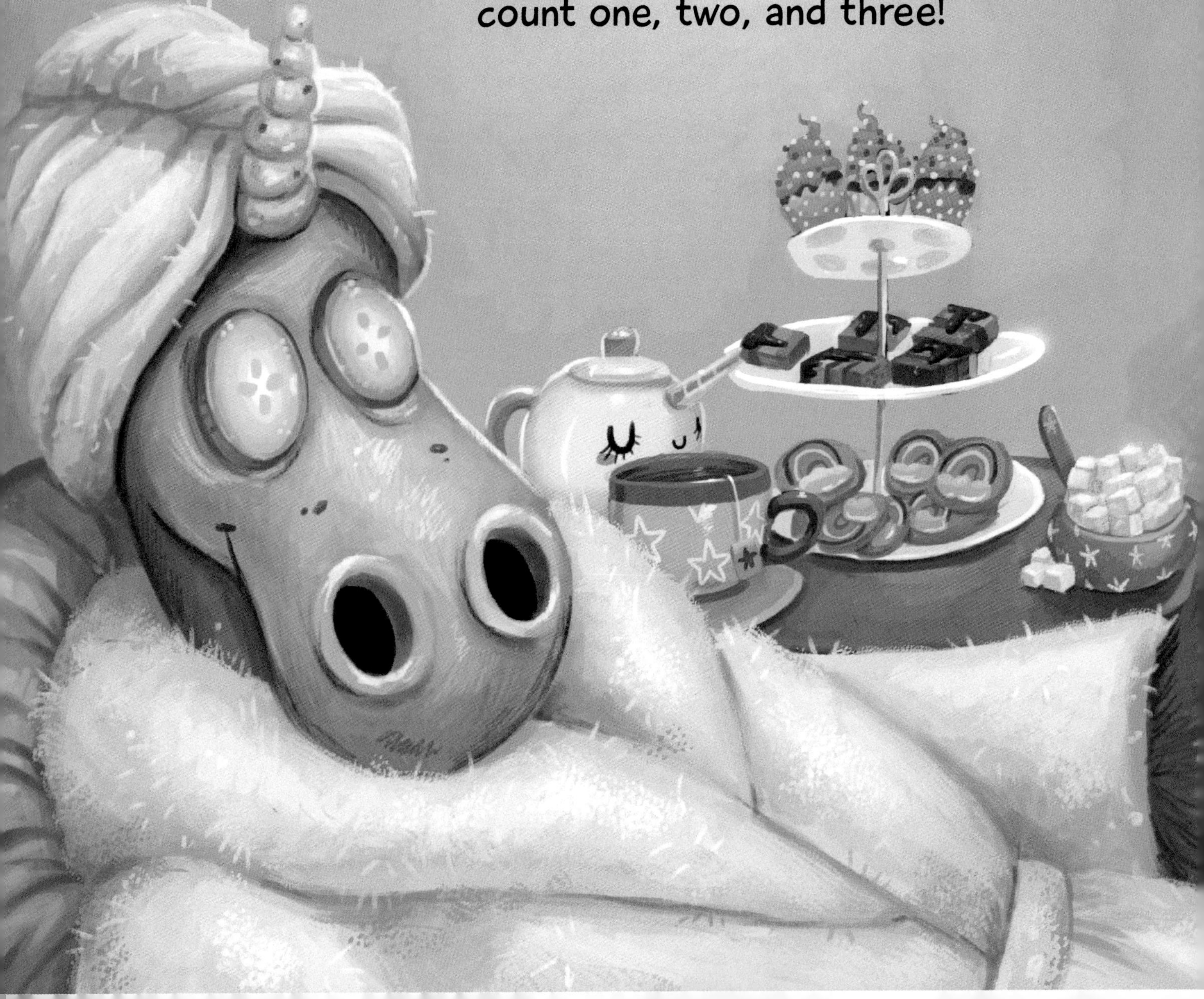

ONE...

TWO...

THREE...

"WOW-EEE!"

Starlight's lips peeled right back with a grin underneath,
and her colorful braces beamed off of her teeth.

She was finally happy.

Her spirits were high....

And she soared through the air
while she painted the sky.

The clouds formed some shapes
of a cool party crew...
with a mermaid, an ostrich –
some fairies showed too!

Then the sun started playing our favorite tunes.
Boy, this had to be one of our best afternoons!

We all marveled at Starlight,
who sparkled and shined.
'Cause she sensed our intentions
were thoughtful and kind.

For, the spirit of kindness will always shine through —
when we all work together to help someone blue.

"It's now time for the cake!" Grandma shouted with glee.
And then, Starlight's horn played "Happy Birthday" for me!

As I blew out my candles,
my breath made a swish.
And I thought long and hard
for my next special wish.

"Hmmm...
soon Christmas will be here,"
I thought to myself...

"Oh! I wish that
dear Santa would
bring me an
ELF!"

Reading is Magical!

Let's have fun answering the who, what, where, why, and how questions below!

1. What was Kat's request on her birthday invitation?
2. Where does Kat live? Can you find her address on her birthday invitation?
3. What were the names of the three unicorns listed on the online ad?
4. What was the name of the unicorn store?
5. Who was the owner of the unicorn store?
6. Why was Starlight a mess when she arrived at Kat's birthday party?
7. How many days did Starlight go without a bath?
8. What did Kat and her party friends do to try to lift Starlight's spirits?
9. What did Starlight have on her teeth?
10. What shapes in the clouds did you see when Starlight soared through the sky?
11. What did Kat wish for at the end of the story?
12. What acts of kindness have you done for someone? How did it make you feel doing something kind for someone else?
13. There are several ostriches in the story, from book 1, Do Not Wish for a Pet Ostrich! Can you count how many ostriches you can find in the story?
14. If you had a unicorn, what name would you give it? Can you draw a picture of your unicorn and explain what makes this unicorn special?
15. If you could make a magical wish for a birthday-themed guest, who would it be?

Dear Reader,

I hope this book brought a smile to your face. If you enjoyed it, please take a moment to leave an honest review on Amazon. If you like silly and fun stories, please check out book 1, *Do Not Wish for a Pet Ostrich!*

Do not forget to send me your artwork and description of your special unicorn! I love to see my readers creativity!

Always find time to smile, sparkle, and shine!

Happy reading. I look forward to hearing from you!

xo,
Sarina

Sarina is available to connect with you for an author visit to schools, libraries, birthday parties, and other special events! Contact her at books@sarinasiebenaler.com.

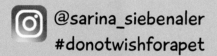

@sarina_siebenaler
#donotwishforapet

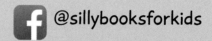

@sillybooksforkids

A free gift for you! Download an educational lesson plan and activities at www.sarinasiebenaler.com. Follow along as we make announcements for future books in this Silly Books for Kids Collection!

Collect them both!

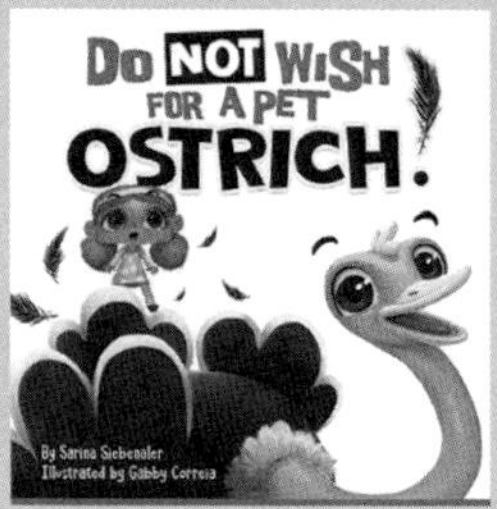

Who will Kat wish for next?
Sign up to know when book 3 is ready for release!

About the Author

Sarina Siebenaler lives in sunny Arizona with her husband, three children, and her rescued Goldendoodle. Her love of poetry, art, and obsession with children's books has inspired her writing journey. She hopes to continue writing children's books to encourage literacy, spark a child's imagination, and help with social and emotional skills. She believes that laughter in picture books encourages and helps motivate reading, as it has with her own three children. Her debut children's book, "Do Not Wish for a Pet Ostrich!" is the first in this collection of story humor. She spends her free time running, hiking, and taking new adventures with her family.

Say hello at www.sarinasiebenaler.com or get social on @sarina_siebenaler or on @sillybooksforkids

About the Illustrator

Gabby Correia has been a self-taught digital artist for nearly ten years with early childhood development qualifications. She resides in the northern suburbs of Cape Town, South Africa. Her artistic talents began with the work of graphic novels, portraits, and advertising. In 2018, she developed a newfound passion for illustrating children's books. She also offers freelance services for personalized caricature portraits. Her creative expression through the art of storytelling in picture books has allowed her to use her imagination to explore the companionship of bringing authors' visions to life. On her time off, she enjoys the beauty of nature with long walks, hiking, and visiting the beach with her boyfriend and her two Jack Russel Terriers.

Say hello at https://nightshadeberry.weebly.com/ or get social on @art_of_nightshadeberry.

Made in the USA
Coppell, TX
16 May 2023

16934442R00026